W9-BGJ-313

First American Edition 1992

Copyright © by William Heinemann Ltd. 1991.
All rights reserved under International and Pan-
American Copyright Conventions. Published in
the United States by Random House, Inc., New
York. Originally published in Great Britain by
William Heinemann Ltd. All publishing rights:
William Heinemann Ltd., London. All television
and merchandising rights licensed by William
Heinemann Ltd. to Britt Allcroft (Thomas) Ltd.
exclusively, worldwide. Library of Congress
Catalog Card Number: 91-62681
ISBN: 0-679-82778-1

Manufactured in Italy
by G. Canale & C. S.p.A. - Borgaro T.se (Turin)
10 9 8 7 6 5 4 3 2

# Thomas's
# BIG BOOK
# of Words

Christopher Awdry

Illustrated by Ken Stott

RANDOM HOUSE
NEW YORK

lighthouse

sea gull

grass

cliffs

ship

seal

life preserver

dock

surfboard

pail

seaweed

pebbles

starfish

tidal pool

crab

After a sunny day by the sea it was time for Polly and her little brother Ben to go home.

Harold the helicopter

flag

buoy

rocks

sailboat

sea

waves

thermos

inflatable tube

bag

shovel

bathing suit

beach towel

sand castle

seashell

beach ball

lamp

poster

VISIT SUNNY
ARLESBURGH

flag

whistle

buffers

conductor

bench

crate

MAIL

steam

dome

TICKET OFFICE

clock

Gordon the big engine

platform

suitcase

hand truck

porter

trunk

mailbags

hatbox

When they were waiting for the train at the big station, they noticed they had lost their pail and shovel.

window.

top hat

lamp

coat

Henry the green engine

chair

Sir Topham Hatt

ink

filing tray

pencil

pen

telephone

letters

desk

wastepaper basket

plant

map of Sodor

ISLAND OF SODOR

timetable

TIMETABLE

| A.M. | P.M |
|------|-----|
| 6-00 | 1-00 |
| 6-30 | 2-15 |
| 7-00 | 3-00 |
| 7-30 | 4-00 |
| 9-00 | 4-3 |
| 9-30 | 5-0 |
| 10-00 | 7-00 |
| 11-30 | 9-00 |

briefcase

filing cabinet

umbrella

planter

umbrella stand

They went to Sir Topham Hatt's office.

"Please, have you seen our pail and shovel?" they asked.

"No," said Sir Topham Hatt, "but try the ticket office."

clock

TIMETABLE

| A.M. | P.M. |
|------|------|
| 6-00 | 1-00 |
| 6-30 | 2-15 |
| 7-00 | 3-00 |
| 7-30 | 4-00 |
| 9-00 | 4-30 |
| 9-30 | 5-00 |
| 10-00 | 7-00 |
| 11-30 | 9-00 |

passenger

price list

PRICES
SINGLE - £5.00
RETURN - £10.00
CHILD £2.50
DOG £1.00
CAT £0.50

files

tickets

season tickets

ticket clerk

cabinet

briefcase

drawers

stool

chair

money

fountain pen

key

cashbox

"Sorry," said the man in the ticket office.
"Try asking at the newsstand."

calendar

jacket

door

manager

safe

station cat

rug

But Polly and Ben were thirsty, so first they went to the station snack shop for a drink. No one there had seen their pail and shovel.

window

Thomas the tank engine

bird

wall

broom

refrigerator

straws

napkins

garbage can

bucket

orangeade

glass

salt    pepper

table

plates

glasses

cans of juice

cups

coffeepot

tea urn

sandwiches

oranges

TEA

burgers

chips

cookies

counter

apples

bananas

cup

fork

saucer

chair

cat

sugar bowl

knife

tree

church

shade

driver

BUS STOP

Bertie the bus

wall

cards

comics

newspapers

candy

15

cash registe

money

pens

tape

rubber bands

salesperson

toys

envelopes

magazines

books

display stand

And the man at the newsstand didn't have them either.

"What about asking at the baggage office?" he said.

pencils

erasers

stool

chocolate

There were lots of suitcases and packages at the baggage office, but no pail and shovel.

shelves

letters

box

scale

bicycle

suitcases

mouse

backpacks

packages

labels

string

clock

Toby the tram engine

rope

lockers

padlock

trunk

crate

duffel bag

teddy bear

umbrella

smoke

smokestack

dome

whistle

Thomas

coupling
hook

rails

boxes

carrots

tomatoes

pears

Suddenly the conductor blew his whistle, and
Mom and Dad bundled Polly and Ben onto
the train for home.

cottage

fields

tree

Thomas

Annie

cow

sheep

gate

pig

stile

fox

They looked out of the window as the train traveled through the countryside.

"Our pail and shovel aren't anywhere," they said sadly.

"Never mind, let's play 'I Spy,'"
said Dad.
"I spy with my little eye four
things beginning with R," said Ben.

bridge

water mill

wheel

oarlock

swan

rowboat

oar

water rat

frog

heron

minnows

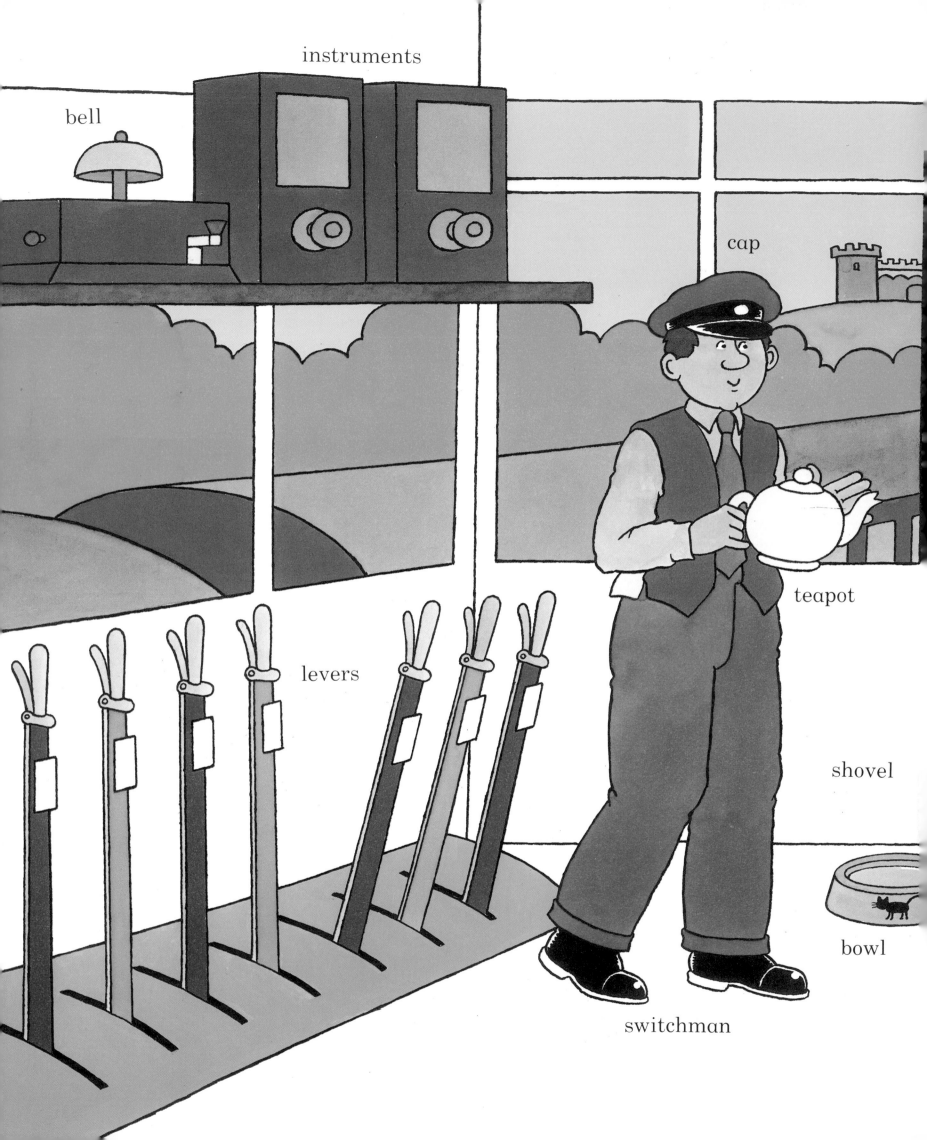

bell

instruments

cap

teapot

levers

shovel

switchman

bowl

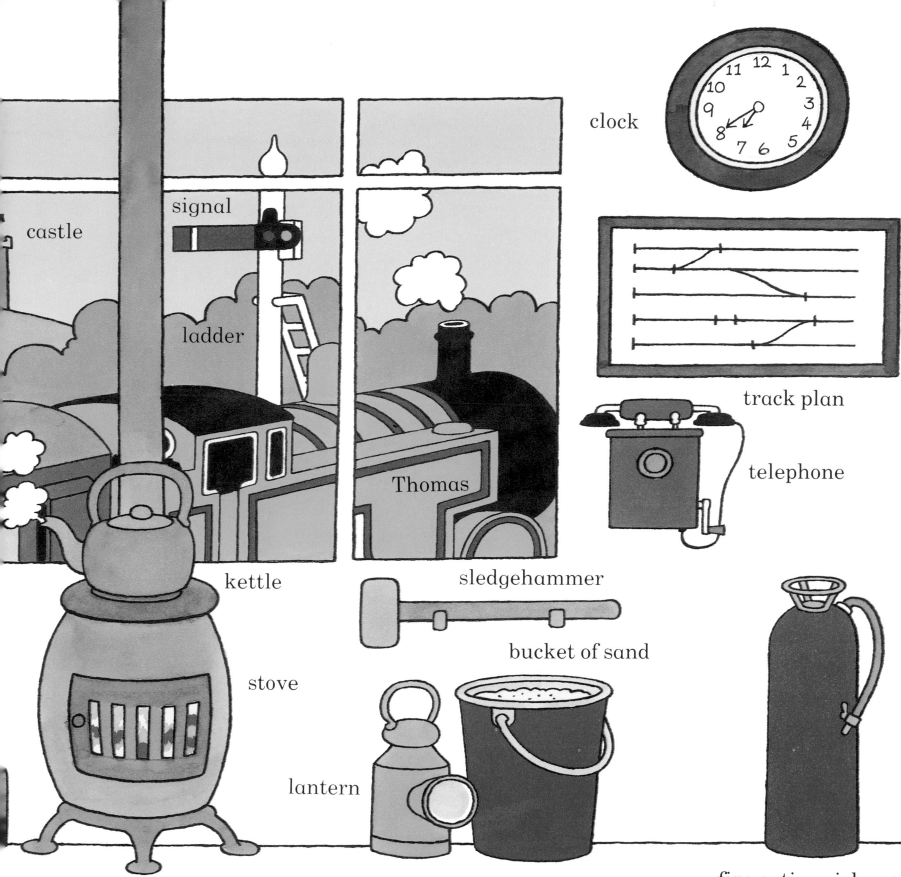

clock

castle

signal

ladder

track plan

Thomas

telephone

kettle

sledgehammer

stove

bucket of sand

lantern

fire extinguisher

The train stopped at the
signal tower.

"I spy with my little eye
something beginning with *K*,"
said Polly, watching the
switchman make himself
a cup of tea.

bird

Percy

Thomas

dog

platform

passenger

"Nearly there," said Mom as they all got ready
to leave the train.

Imagine their surprise when a conductor handed
them their pail and shovel on the way out.

"Thomas's driver found it on the platform
with the mailbags just as the train was about to
leave," he said.

"Thank you, Thomas," called Polly and Ben.

And Thomas smiled as he puffed away.